Rehearsal's Off!

Rehearsal's Off!

George Booth

AVON
PUBLISHERS OF BARD, CAMELOT AND DISCUS BOOKS

AVON BOOKS
A division of
The Hearst Corporation
959 Eighth Avenue
New York, New York 10019
Copyright © 1976 by George Booth
Published by arrangement with Dodd, Mead & Company.
Library of Congress Catalog Card Number: 76-41381
ISBN: 0-380-01719-9

First Avon Printing, September, 1977

AVON TRADEMARK REG. U.S. PAT. OFF. AND IN
OTHER COUNTRIES, MARCA REGISTRADA, HECHO EN
U.S.A.

Printed in the U.S.A.

To Dione

An account of the not too significant chain
of little crises in the life of a struggling Missouri artist

GEORGE WAS BORN June 28, 1926, to a pair of amateur pedagogues. His first movements were open hands reaching out beckoningly into space. The doctor said, "I never saw a new-born youngster do that before."

At one and one-half years he and his older brother Gaylord disappeared. Maw Maw went anxiously in search of them. Gaylord was waddling and George was crawling in the dirt. She asked them where they were going and they·said, "To Grandma's house." Grandma lived thirty miles away.

While Dad was supervising classroom and other school activities, George would tightly grasp his pant legs with both hands and bounce and bob along from place to place. The pupils called him "The Shadow."

In high school he worked diligently to make the football team. The coach trained him carefully and called on him to make the opening kickoff. George gave a mighty lunge and swoosh, missed the ball, and threw his knee out of place. Thus ended his football career.

On the farm he tried engineering. We'd supply shovels, rakes, hoes, spades, axes, and pitchforks and send him to the work site. Soon he'd come back with broken tools. Never did find a handle that would survive his strength. And so his agri-business career was terminated.

George graduated from high school (1944) at Fairfax, Missouri, and was soon called for military service. He enlisted in the Marines, trained at Parris Island and Camp Lejeune, and was shipped to Hawaii for maneuvers. George was on Maui when orders came to report to Pearl Harbor. His "spec" number showed that he was a Linotype operator. (He had learned how to use the Linotype as an apprentice in high school.) A colonel had written a book and George was picked to set the type.

While taking a coffee break, he was drawing a picture of the Colonel to entertain his office mates. Unknown to the group the Colonel had joined the circle to see what was going on. After the picture was completed, the Colonel ordered George to report to his office. With some apprehension George did so. Said the Colonel, "There's an army plane leaving for Stateside within the hour. Get your gear together and be on it. I'm assigning you to the *Leatherneck* staff in Washington, D.C." And so a cartooning career was launched.

After George completed his first enlistment, he was mustered out, went to Chicago Academy of Fine Arts, and was called back into the service to retrain for duty in Korea. As he readied to board ship for Korea, orders came through for him to return to Washington as a staff sergeant on the Leatherneck publication.

He completed his second enlistment, attended Corcoran Art School in Washington, D.C., and Adelphi College on Long Island.

George worked for Bill Communications in New York City for about eight years and then decided to do free-lance cartooning. He finally got his big toe in the door at the *New Yorker*, where his dogs, cats, and miserable human beings have provided the means for his survival ever since. Along the way, inspiration and help have been supplied in abundance by George's talented wife Dione and his quizzical daughter, Sarah Nell.

DAD

"*I do apologize, Rinehart. The cat has never bitten anyone previously.*"

"Arthur, if you were doing undercover work for the CIA, you'd tell me . . . wouldn't you?"

"I'm with Governor Carey. 'The days of wine and roses are over.'"

"Old Whittington figures if he makes it through March he's good for the rest of the year."

"The trustees feel the Reverend Dr. Clapsattle does not harmonize with the edifice."

"*The boys located a short in your high-voltage wire, Mr. Bates.*"

"You twitched and whinnied all night!"

BOOTH

"*Mouth-to-mouth resuscitation is out. . . . Perhaps a dog biscuit would help.*"

BOOTH

"This is your anchorman, John Moore, saying, 'That's all there is. There is no more.' Until tomorrow at the same time, when there will be more."

BOOTH

"There are few moments in music so thrilling as when Brucie
and Mrs. Ritterhouse start riffing in tandem."

"*Sticks and stones may break my bones, but moussaka will never harm me.*"

"Why don't you two get acquainted?"

BOOTH

"Now hear this! Mr. Wetzel is prepared to comply with state and fed-
eral emission-control standards if and when they become effective. Until
such time, Mr. Wetzel will continue to indulge himself in the manner
to which he has become accustomed. That is all."

"*George Stoner is here from Terre Haute. He and Henry are talking over old times.*"

"Do you have a dinner jacket, sir?"

Unidog commuter balloon

1975 Whippet-eight

Three-dog runabout

details of brake

Dogs answering to "Gee!" and "Haw" are preferable to steering harness

New York City twenty-dog bus

NEW YORK CITY 20·DOG BUS

details of brake

Hoopmobile

Hoopmobile-motor principle (see below)

Hundswagen

SA-118

BOOTH

"That niche used to be the cigarette-machine niche, then it was the water-cooler niche, and now it's Mr. Pendleton's niche."

"The Schoonover sisters' cotton batting is loose."

"...and Zimmerman, down there on the end, is a leg man ... but don't worry about it, Honey ... there ain't been a breeze in any of their sails in the last twenty-five years."

"*He owed a lot of back taxes.*"

"Our main bank is right near your home, and we have fifteen other handy branches with all the latest push-button systems. We'll give you top interest rates and lollipops on your 'rainy-day' savings account. You can also have a safe-deposit box that no one but you is allowed to open. You'll get free 'stop-and-bank' souvenirs, such as little silver Empire State Buildings and Abraham Lincolns. There is a brand-new playground next to your bank, and you'll get a chance to win one of the grand sweepstakes prizes —hi-fi stereo, color television, or two weeks for two in Mexico City."

BOOTH.

"We covered His Majesty with flannels but he gat no heat. . . . We summoned the Queen but still he gat no heat. . . . Then we brought forth a sweet young virgin to nurture him and now he's beginning to gat a little heat."

BOOTH

"We did everything modern science could do, but there are
some things we just haven't learned."

"Did you woof?"

"Write about dogs!"

"It's time to pay the fiddler."

BOOTH

"*It's blend of ground meats and tasty gravies appetizingly poured over a shingle.*"

"How time flies! It was just thirty years ago tonight that you first ran me a hot bath—right here in this very tub."

"Now, in your twilight time, brave warrior Oolak, in consideration of your forty-three years of courageous and devoted service, we the chiefs have decided to let you run for it. . . ."

"From the top—'Watermelon Man.' Let's sock it out and give Mrs. Ritterhouse a chance to really cook!"

"*I haven't said anything up to now, but now I'm going to speak my piece. I think New York City had better get back to the good old buy-now-pay-as-you-go days, and pretty darn soon or there's going to be trouble. That's what I think!*"

"Mr. Pittman spent the late sixties hunkering down. Then, in the early seventies, he made an effort to get it all together. These past months, he's been trying to find the handle."

BOOTH

"You have a healthy, eight-pound baby boy, Mrs. McKeever.... Get up!"

"*I'm so hungry, I could eat a bear!*"

BOOTH

BOOTH

"I've got an idea for a story: Gus and Ethel live on Long Island, on the North Shore. He works sixteen hours a day writing fiction. Ethel never goes out, never does anything except fix Gus sandwiches, and in the end she becomes a nympho-lesbo-killer-whore. Here's your sandwich."

CLUNK!

CLUNK!

CLUNK!

BOOTH

"He said, 'Tell the Telephone Company to go fly a kite.'"

BOOTH

BOC

"Let's take the Andantino in C again . . . this time without the cat!"

"*As one citizen to another, Mr. Crutchfield, I suggest you make a run for the border.*"

"That, honey, is probably an end."

"Take it from the beginning. Act One. 'Gypsy.' 'May We Entertain You?'
And this time, Mrs. Ritterhouse, <u>without</u> the Baby June split."

"*It's getting harder and harder to find a bargain these days, but guess what I picked up today for five dollars and forty-nine cents. An Australian flame pea!*"

"We've had our chief mechanic on her for the good part of two days but she still doesn't want to turn over. True, she was running when you brought her in yesterday morning but then machines are like man. They have their alpha and they have their omega. It appears we are witness, Mr. Trowbridge, to your old whoopee's omega."

"*Edgar, please run down to the shopping center right away, and get some milk and cat food. Don't get canned tuna, or chicken, or liver or any of those awful combinations. Shop around and get a surprise. The pussies like surprises.*"

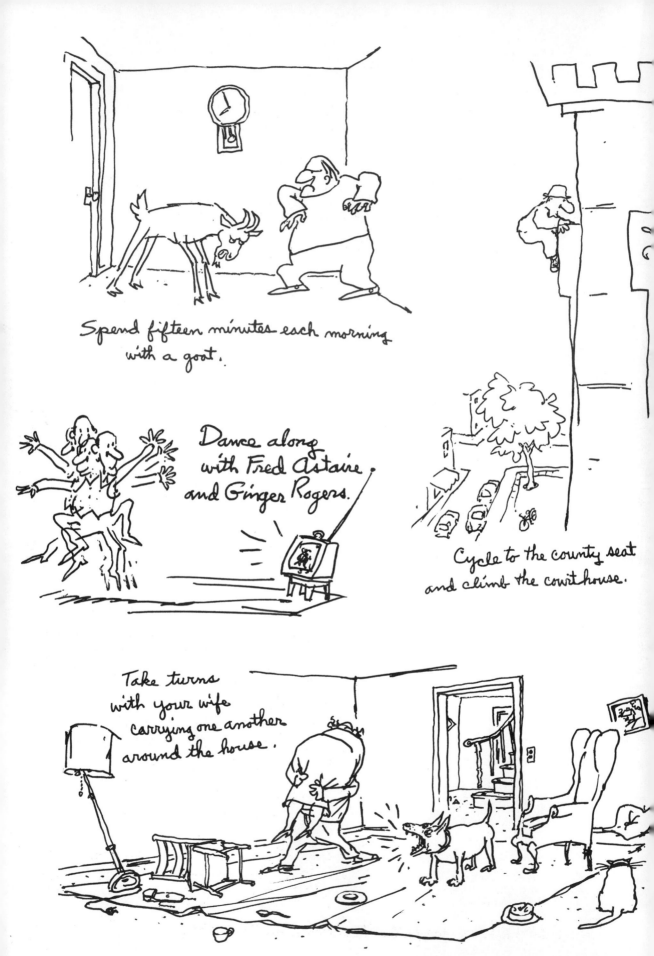

Spend fifteen minutes each morning with a goat.

Dance along with Fred Astaire and Ginger Rogers.

Cycle to the county seat and climb the court house.

Take turns with your wife carrying one another around the house.

KEEPING FIT

Run through the parking lot once a day and touch every car.

Climb stairs pretending that only every fourth step is safe.

Imagine you have infiltrated enemy territory and proceed to your office under hostile fire.

Hop to work on one foot. Hop home on the other.

"Mrs. Henry H. Hamilton III drove down from the Ridge today in her big fine car ... then she gets out with her fur piece and diamonds and looks around. She proceeds to tell me that *my* dishes are *not* antiques and that they are *chipped* ... that *she* could get a full set of the exact same pattern, without any chipped places, for *less* money, at Bloomingdale's in New York City. ... So I tells the son of a bitch 'Why don't you get your ass over to Bloomingdales!'"

BOOTH

"My name is Virgil and I've got the only plane in these parts
. . . so you may as well fly me."

BOOTH

"Hon, read me something from Jack Anderson—blowing-the-lid-off-wise."

BOOTH

BOOTH

"I want more staccato from the clarinet, more pizzicato from the strings, and less booze from the trombones."

"One day at a time, Ethel, I take it one day at a time. So far this year, it has been the usual assortment of useless junk. Last week, he located a dump scow, and he spent all _this_ week dragging a 1929 Ford engine block out of the river. Sunday, he made himself sick—thought he had a pirate's gewgaw, but when the mud came off, it turned out to be an ice-cream-freezer crank. I take it one day at a time, Ethel, one day at a time."

"*I feel idiotically happy today.*"

BOOTH

"See there! . . . The System *does* work."

*(1) Burglar raises bedroom window, which (2) lowers
bale of hay; (3) elephant sees hay, (4) steps forward
onto greased runway, and (5) burglar is frightened
away by (6) charging elephant. (Pat. Pending)*

*"I'm sorry to interrupt the più mosso, but Mrs. Patterson
informs me the cat has passed away."*

"I'm an American taxpayer! I've already been ripped off!"

БООТН

"*It's sixteen hundred dollars for August, including gas, electricity, maintenance, beach sticker, and old Mrs. Pennington up in the attic.*"

"*And that's the opinion of Herman Fletcher. This is Herman Fletcher, signing off.*"

BOOTH

"What worries me about the will is the way he laughed when he passed away."

BOOTH

"*Putty took a wife. Her name was Pussums, and she bore him Little Gentleman, Biddy Boo, Savor Tooth, Fluffy, Harry Cat, and Caesar. Then Little Gentleman begat Little Gentleman II and Friday and Twinkle Toes and Possum Tail and . . .*"

BOOTH

"This hurts us more than it will hurt you, Mr. Lippincott. The Internal
Revenue Service has no previous record of a public dipping."

"Immediately on your left, as you leave, you will see a little old lady begging for coins. She is the Museum Director . . ."

"*Your mother is off her rocker and the cats are at her.*"

"That country rock group in apartment eight-C is looking for a deep voice to go dip-doo-ba-dip-dip-dip-badoo..."

BOOTH

"Today I'm going to work from outside in, then tomorrow from inside out.
It seems like when I start from inside I never get out."

"*Lecture time!*"

"I'm a biggie in the world of finance. I'm even a big biggie. But, Janice, I'm a very lonesome biggie."

THE
COLONIAL
ELECTRIC COMPANY
announces
THE CONSTRUCTION OF
ANOTHER DAMNED
POWER PLANT
ON THIS SITE

BOOTH

BOOTH

"Yesterday, Harold decided to (quote) run the old jalopy until the wheels fall off (unquote) and this morning, at fifteen minutes past eight, they did."

"*Pettijohn, we expected you to perk up in the fourth quarter. Instead you have sagged a notch or two.*"

"Our computerized telecommunications system is higgledy-piggledy."

"Rehearsal's off! Our first violinist was apprehended early this morning poaching clams in Great South Bay! The authorities have confiscated her rake and long tongs!"